ADOPTION CERTIFICATE

PET NAME: PETUNIA

COLOUR: BRIGHT RED

FAVOURITE FOOD: DINO CRUNCH

THIS PET T-REX BELONGS TO:

....

For Pamella,
with love and ink.

ORCHARD BOOKS
First published in Great Britain in 2020 by The Watts Publishing Group
1 3 5 7 9 10 8 6 4 2
Text and illustrations © Fabi Santiago 2020
The moral rights of the author have been asserted.
All rights reserved.
A CIP catalogue record for this book is available from the British Library.
HB ISBN 978 1 40835 347 9 • PB ISBN 978 1 40835 349 3
Printed and bound in China

MIX
Paper from
responsible sources
FSC® C104740
FSC
www.fsc.org

Orchard Books, an imprint of Hachette Children's Group,
part of The Watts Publishing Group Limited
Carmelite House, 50 Victoria Embankment, London EC4Y 0DZ
An Hachette UK Company
www.hachette.co.uk
www.hachettechildrens.co.uk

FABI SANTIAGO

MY PET T-REX

ORCHARD

Congratulations! You've just adopted your first pet. And what an excellent choice: a **T-REX.**

T-rexes make great pets. They **DON'T** shed fur. They **DON'T** scratch. They **DON'T** bark, and they certainly **DON'T** run round in circles trying to bite their own tails.

Petunia, will you say hello to your new owner?

Hi, Petunia, I'm Kiki.

ROAR!

Terrific! She really likes you, Kiki.

Now, looking after a pet is a serious business. Are you ready?

The first thing you need to do is introduce

your pet T-rex to her new home.

Mum and Dad will be delighted!

NO ONE can resist a friendly T-rex.

Your pet T-rex will need **LOTS** of love and attention to help her settle in. You will need to:

keep her **CLEAN** . . .

and **COMFORTABLE** . . .

and **FEED** her regularly. Petunia will eat her own weight in Dino Crunch every day.

You'll also need to **CLEAR UP** after her.

Gross!

Well, I never said having a pet T-rex would be easy, did I?

Pets need to make regular trips to the **vet**,

and T-rexes are no exception.

You'll also need to give your pet T-rex some

TRAINING.

Try teaching Petunia the basics:

STAY!

SIT!

Oh dear, Petunia! That's **NOT** what you were meant to fetch.

It's clear your pet T-rex has **LOTS** of energy.
She'll need plenty of **EXERCISE** and
somewhere safe to play. Try the park . . .

DINO PARK

PRIMORDIAL PUDDLES ←

PTERODACTYLS →

but be careful of **OTHER PETS**...

and watch out . . .

for those

primordial . . .

SPLASH

SPLASH

SPLASH

SPLASH

ROAR!

What's that? You don't want a pet T-rex any more?

NO!

I know they're hard work, Kiki. But surely you're not going to give up now? Petunia needs you . . .

PETUNIA?

Yes, pets can be
very sensitive . . .

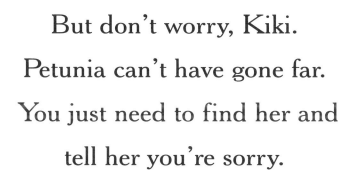

But don't worry, Kiki.
Petunia can't have gone far.
You just need to find her and
tell her you're sorry.

Try calling for her and bringing a bag of delicious treats.

Have you looked in all
her favourite places?

Don't give up, Kiki!

Ah! Look who's back! See?
There was no need to worry.

And it looks like Petunia's got

SOMETHING FOR YOU.

Petunia!

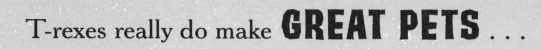

T-rexes really do make **GREAT PETS** . . .

. . . don't they?